Just a Box

Written by
Laura Appleton-Smith

Illustrated by
Keinyo White

Laura Appleton-Smith holds a degree in English from Middlebury College. Laura is a primary school teacher who has combined her talents in creative writing with her experience in early childhood education to create *Books to Remember*. She lives in New Hampshire with her husband, Terry.

Keinyo White is a graduate of the Rhode Island School of Design with a B.F.A. in illustration. He currently produces children's books and freelance illustrations from his studio in Los Angeles. This is his sixth book from Flyleaf Publishing.

A Book to Remember™
Published by Flyleaf Publishing

For orders or information, contact us at **(800) 449-7006**.
Please visit our website at **www.flyleafpublishing.com**

Eighth Edition 2/20
Library of Congress Catalog Card Number: 2005911123
Softcover ISBN-13: 978-1-929262-49-6
Printed and bound in the USA
243081021A7

Anita and Ramon like to help their Papa do projects. One project they like to do is help Papa at the dump.

One day a man at the dump had a big box.
It was the biggest box that Ramon and Anita
had ever seen!

The man was just getting set to drop the box
in the dumpster when Anita asked if she could have it.
"Yes," he said, "it is just a box."

Ramon and Anita lifted the box into the back of Papa's pickup truck.

Papa helped to strap the box in.

Back at home, the kids dragged the box
onto the back deck.

Mama asked, "What the dickens do you plan
to make with that big box?"

First, Anita ran and got the mop to put up a mast.
Ramon hung up a blanket as a flag.

9

Ramon and Anita went on a trip to cross the Atlantic.
It was not just a box. It was a ship!

Next, they flipped the box and lifted the top flap.

It was not just a box. It was a bus. Anita and Ramon
went to Africa and spotted lots of animals.

Ramon flipped the box and Anita got helmets.

Blast off! It was not just a box. It was the cockpit of a rocket ship. The kids blasted off on a cosmic trip to visit the sun.

After dinner Ramon and Anita asked Mama and Papa if they could camp in the box.

Mama and Papa said, "Yes, that will be fun."

16

The kids propped up the flaps.

They filled the bottom of the box with blankets.

It was not just a box. It was a tent to camp in.

As they slept there was a "drip, drip, drip"
on the top of the box.

The box was getting wet. It was drizzling.
It was not just drizzling. It was a tempest!

The kids grabbed their
stuffed animals and
their blankets and ran!

The next day the kids inspected the box.
It had melted into a wet lump on the back deck.

"That is sad," Mama said.
"It is OK, Mama," Anita said. "It was just a box."

24

"We can get a box on the next trip to the dump," Ramon said. "And it will be even better than the last box!"

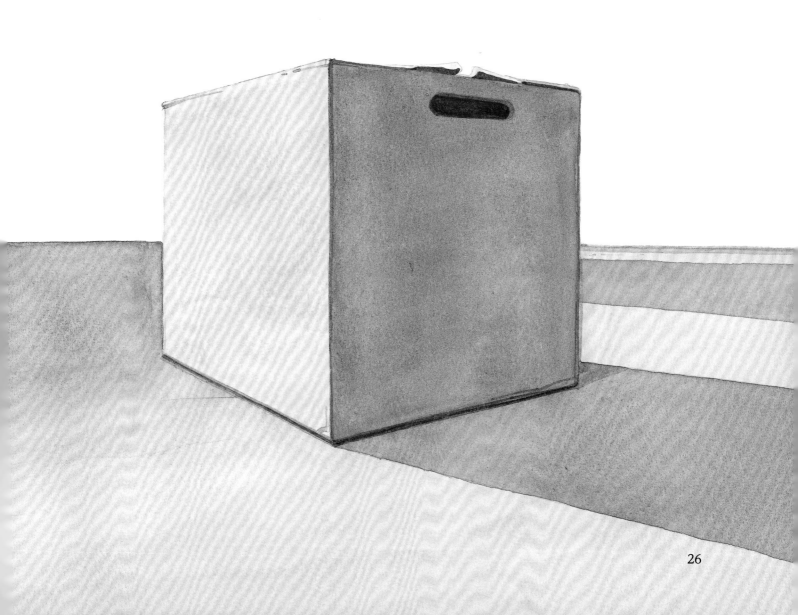

Prerequisite Skills

Single consonants and short vowels
Final double consonants **ff**, **gg**, **ll**, **nn**, **ss**, **tt**, **zz**
Consonant /k/ **ck**
/ng/ **n[k]**
Consonant digraphs /ng/ **ng**, /th/ **th**, /hw/ **wh**
Schwa /ə/ **a**, **e**, **i**, **o**, **u**
Long /ē/ **ee**, **y**
r-Controlled /ûr/ **er**
/ô/ **al**, **all**
/ul/ **le**
/d/ or /t/ –**ed**

Target Letter-Sound Correspondence

Foundational Skills
Consolidation

Story Puzzle Words

Anita	Papa's
Mama	Ramon
onto	ship
Papa	

High-Frequency Puzzle Words

be	one
could	put
day	said
do	she
even	their
first	there
have	they
he	to
home	was
into	we
like	what
make	you
of	

a	bottom	ever	in	OK	tempest
Africa	box	filled	inspected	on	tent
after	bus	flag	is	pickup	than
and	camp	flap	it	plan	that
animals	can	flaps	just	project	the
as	cockpit	flipped	kids	projects	top
asked	cosmic	fun	last	propped	trip
at	cross	get	lifted	ran	truck
Atlantic	deck	getting	lots	rocket	up
back	dickens	got	lump	sad	visit
better	dinner	grabbed	man	seen	went
big	dragged	had	mast	set	wet
biggest	drip	helmets	melted	slept	when
blanket	drizzling	help	mop	spotted	will
blankets	drop	helped	next	strap	with
blast	dump	hung	not	stuffed	yes
blasted	dumpster	if	off	sun	